Whiteblack the Penguin Sees the World

Whiteblack the Penguin Sees the World

MARGRET & H. A. REY

Houghton Mifflin Company
Boston 2000

Library of Congress Cataloging-in-Publication Data

Rey, Margret.
Whiteblack the penguin sees the world / by Margret Rey ; illustrated by H.A. Rey.
p.   cm.
Summary: In search of new stories for his radio program, Whiteblack the penguin
sets out on a journey and has some interesting adventures.
ISBN 0-618-07389-2
[1. Penguins — Fiction. 2. Voyages and travels — Fiction. 3. Animals — Fiction.] I. Title.
PZ7.R33Wf   2000
[E] — dc21
00-023196

Manufactured in the United States of America
WOZ 10 9 8 7 6 5 4 3 2 1

WHITEBLACK THE PENGUIN was worried. He was the Chief Storyteller on Station W-O-N-S. Spelled backwards it read S-N-O-W, the radio station for all Penguinland. And he had run out of stories.

"I guess I'll take a vacation and travel," he said. "Travelers always have lots of stories."

His friends Seal and Polar Bear agreed.

"But you'll need a boat," said Seal. "You can't swim all the time. I'll give you half of an old seal skin. It will make a fine boat."

"And I," said Polar Bear, "I'll give you rope made from the hair of my last winter's fur. Ropes are always useful."

"That's wonderful," said Whiteblack. "Besides, I've always wanted a boat and a rope."

So he began to build the boat, and with all the family helping, it was finished in no time. Whiteblack was ready for his trip.

Everybody waved farewell to him.

"Come back with plenty of stories!" barked Seal.

"And bring us nice presents!" said Polar Bear.

"I promise!" shouted Whiteblack. "Good-bye!"

The boat moved away from the shore, and soon he was alone on the wide blue ocean.

Hours went by and not much happened. Sometimes Whiteblack swam pulling the boat behind him, and sometimes he sat in the boat using his flippers as paddles.

"I thought traveling was more exciting," he said. Feeling bored, he fell asleep.

CRACK! He awoke to a heavy shock. His boat had hit an iceberg! It was sinking fast. "I hate to lose my boat," he said, "but at least this is a story for my radio show. Besides, I've always wanted to be in an accident."

He untied the
rope just as the boat
went under. He then
tied it around his middle
and swam on.

After a while Whiteblack
saw smoke on the horizon:
there was a cruiser steaming
straight toward him.

"I'll go on board and look at
this ship," he said.

When the cruiser was close enough, he lassoed a gun and climbed on board.

Everything aboard the cruiser was clean and shiny, and Whiteblack was pleased. On deck was one of those famous human beings he had heard so much about!

"I've always wanted to see a man, but I thought he'd look more unusual," Whiteblack said. "Why, he looks just like me! White shirt, dark coat, and he walks on two legs. Only he's got lovely bright buttons on his jacket. I'll go ask him to let me have a few for my Sunday suit."

Just then the officer and some sailors discovered the little penguin and started chasing him. He ran away as fast as he could and hid in the muzzle of a big gun.

"I hope I'm safe here," he thought. "It's a nice cool place for a *long* nap."

The next morning the sailors started practicing with the gun where Whiteblack was sleeping. BOOM! He went through the air like a thunderbolt, and miles away he dived into the sea.

"This is a *real* story for my radio show!" he said when he came up. "Besides, I've always wanted to fly."

He saw land in the distance and swam ashore.

"This must be a foreign country." He climbed up the beach. "I suppose it's full of stories for my radio show. Besides, I've always wanted to visit a foreign country."

The place was quite different from Penguinland. There was no snow or ice, but there were bright flowers and fresh green plants everywhere. The air was warm, a little too warm for Whiteblack's taste.

But look at the two big white balls lying there! They couldn't be snowballs . . . or could they?

"Perhaps footballs," he thought. "Besides, I've always wanted to play football." He kicked one ball with his foot.

CRICK! The ball broke in two and out came a baby ostrich.

"Thanks for letting me out of the egg," he squeaked. "Won't you please get my brother out, too?"

So Whiteblack hit the second egg and another baby ostrich appeared.

"I've always wanted to see baby ostriches come out of their eggs," Whiteblack said. "It's a very rare experience and a fine story for my radio show."

That moment Father and Mother Ostrich arrived. "What a pleasant surprise," they said. "Won't you accept a little present?" Mother Ostrich gave him a lovely mirror, and Father Ostrich produced a roller skate.

"Thanks," said Whiteblack. "Now I must go because I'm on a trip, collecting stories for my radio show."

"Wait," said Father Ostrich. "The desert is hard to travel for somebody with such short legs — pardon me for saying so. I'll give you a letter of introduction to my friend the camel. He'll let you ride on his back."

Whiteblack took the letter and walked into the desert. It was like the beach in Penguinland, only warmer. Soon he met the camel.

The camel was very glad to have company, for the desert is such a lonely place. "I provide the ferry service across the desert," the camel said, "and I charge a small fee, but because of that letter I shall carry you for free."

The camel knelt down and Whiteblack climbed on its back. "Another good story for my radio show," he said. "Besides, I've always wanted to ride on a camel."

At first Whiteblack liked the ride, but after a while he had a funny feeling in his stomach.

With every step the camel's back moved up and down, up and down, and he felt he was going to be seasick. "This would *not* make a good story for my radio show," he thought, "and besides, I *never* wanted to be seasick. Penguins are not *supposed* to be seasick, ever!"

Finally he could not stand it anymore. He asked the camel to please let him off.

Now he had to walk through the hot desert again, for hours and hours.

"I wish I were home," he sighed. "Besides, I've never wanted to be lost in a desert. I must get out of here somehow." Suddenly he had an idea. He picked up a stick and with his rope he tied it to the roller skate. It made a perfect scooter! It even had a rearview mirror.

He rolled along smoothly all the way to the end of the desert.

"Now I've got enough stories for my radio show," he decided. "I want to go home. If I only knew which way to go. Why, there's a plane over there. Maybe there's somebody who can tell me how to get back to Penguinland."

And there was! An explorer was quite surprised to see the little penguin. "I'm leaving tomorrow," he said, "and I can give you a lift."

The explorer made a little carrier for Whiteblack. And because no animals were allowed inside the plane, the carrier was fastened on top.

"I've always wanted to ride on top of an airplane," said Whiteblack. "Now I'm on my way home!"

The plane took off and flew over towns and rivers and fields and forests and finally it reached the ocean.

"It's getting cooler," thought Whiteblack. "I can feel we are coming closer to Penguinland. I must try to have a look. Besides, I've always wanted to have a look at Penguinland from the air."

He managed to open the door of his carrier and walked out to have a better view.

He bent over and SWOOSH! Down he went, headfirst, and SPLASH! he plumped into the sea.

When he recovered from his fall he looked around. He was curious. There were fish right and left and everywhere; he had never seen so many fish in his life.

Suddenly he and all the fish were lifted out of the water. He had fallen into a fishing net, and the net was being pulled in. Together with everybody else, Whiteblack was dumped into the hold of a fishing boat.

"Not a bad place," he said to himself. "Lots of fish, lots of ice, just the right temperature. Now I can make up for all the meals I've missed during my trip."

So he had ten breakfasts, ten lunches, ten dinners, and ten suppers, all in one, and every course was fish. He was just ready for a nap when he heard a fisherman upstairs say, "Over there lies Penguinland!"

Penguinland! He was almost home and yet he had no present for his friends. "I must bring *something*," he said. "What can I do?" And then a wonderful idea came to him.

At night when everybody was asleep he climbed on deck. He took one of the big nets that were hung up to dry and jumped into the sea.

His idea worked! As he swam toward Penguinland, dragging the net behind him, fish were caught in it. Soon the net became quite heavy. "I don't mind," he thought. "I'm on my way home, with stories to tell and a *marvelous* present!"

The morning came and he could see the shores of Penguinland far away, but the net was so heavy now that he hardly made any headway. "I *must* get home with my present," he panted. "I MUST!"

But his strength was almost gone. He would have to let the net go and come home empty-handed. He just had to give up! Tears were coming to his eyes . . .

"Whiteblack! Hello,
Whiteblack!" shouted a happy
voice. It was Seal, his good friend
Seal, who came rushing through the waves to help him. "I've been
looking out for you every day. I'm *so* glad you are back! What a
marvelous present you brought!" And he took the heavy load from
Whiteblack.

HURRAH! There was a big crowd on the beach to welcome the famous traveler. That same day they had an enormous party with mountains of fish for everybody. Whiteblack had a special radio show on Station W-O-N-S, and he had to tell all his stories over and over again.

And out of snow his friends built a big monument and wrote on it: WHITEBLACK, THE HERO OF PENGUINLAND.

And since in Penguinland the snow never melts, the monument is still there. You can go yourself and see it.

PUBLISHER'S NOTE

The publication of Margret and H. A. Rey's books has long been one of the most dramatic stories of the twentieth century, and the discovery of *Whiteblack the Penguin Sees the World* for publication continues their amazing saga. Many readers already know their history as recounted by critic Leonard Marcus in *The Original Curious George:* "A self-taught artist, Hans Augusto Rey (1898–1977), and his Bauhaus-trained wife and collaborator, Margret (1906–1996), were German Jews who married in Brazil in 1935. After founding the first advertising agency in Rio de Janeiro, they returned to Europe in 1936. They lived in Paris until June 14, 1940, leaving just hours before the German army entered the city. Fleeing by bicycle with their winter coats and four picture books strapped to the racks (including the watercolors and a draft of *Curious George*—then called *Fifi*), they crossed the French border into Spain, hopped a train for Lisbon, then sailed to Brazil. There Hans's Brazilian citizenship and the Roosevelt Good Neighbor Policy eased their passage to the United States."

The Reys eventually went to New York, in October of 1940, and Grace Hogarth, who was the founder of Houghton Mifflin's children's book department, visited them and drew up a four-book contract, a rare item in those days. Those four titles—*Curious George, Cecily G. and the 9 Monkeys*, and two lift-the-flap books (*How Do You Get There?* and *Anybody at Home?*)—remain staples of the Houghton Mifflin children's list to this day. *Curious George* itself, within fifteen years, became the backbone of the list and has delighted several generations of children.

Two years after Margret Rey's death, in 1998, her friend and literary executor, Lay Lee Ong, undertook the year-long task of pulling together all of the Reys' books, sketchbooks, correspondence, and memorabilia to be sent to the de Grummond Collection at the University of Southern Mississippi, in Hattiesburg. Lena de Grummond, the mastermind behind the collection, had written to Hans Rey in the 1950s, asking him for a small drawing to share with his fans. The Reys continued to send more original material, and eventually Margret decided to will all their papers and files to the collection. Dee Jones, curator extraordinaire of the collection, approached all the cataloguing, filing, sorting, and compiling in her usual meticulous manner. With such a rich array of material, she then pulled together an extensive exhibit, set up a lecture schedule in conjunction with it, and invited Lay Lee Ong and me to come open the exhibit.

In October 1999, as I viewed the exhibit for the first time, I noticed a case enclosing an intriguing watercolor drawing labeled "Unpublished work of H. A. Rey." Within a few minutes, Dee produced the original sketches for a book. On the jacket illustration was the address line "Propriété de l'auteur H. A. Rey, Paris." What followed were the adventures of Whiteblack the Penguin, illustrated with Rey's glorious watercolors. Suddenly I realized that the Reys had clearly brought a fifth book from Paris.

Correspondence in the files further indicated that the Reys had been talking to Ursula Nordstrom at Harper and Row about publishing the book. She had sent it back to them for a revision, which they had worked on. But for some reason—possibly because they started to create other books or another Curious George book—they never resubmitted the manuscript. It sat for many years in the Reys' home. According to Ong, Margret would say from time to time that she thought *Whiteblack* was one of their best books, but no one had ever published it. This statement particularly amazed me since I had sat many times on Margret's couch and asked her, "Margret, is there anything else you'd like me to take a look at?"

Whiteblack the Penguin Sees the World was conceived in 1937, when Hans was working in the Brazilian Pavilion at the Paris World's Fair. He was stationed across from a penguin exhibit, and he took great delight in drawing these fanciful creatures and creating characters out of them. Eventually, he and Margret drafted the entire saga of Whiteblack the Penguin; later, they strapped it onto a bicycle and fled Paris.

Now, sixty-three years later, *Whiteblack the Penguin Sees the World* is being published for the first time. A superb example of H. A. Rey's early work, the book has been executed in his French watercolor style and demonstrates the childlike understanding and humor that both Hans and Margret brought to their books. It seems serendipitous that a new book by the Reys graces Houghton's children's list in the year 2000. We are grateful to Dee Jones and the de Grummond Collection for their fine exhibit and for lending us the art for the book. We are also indebted to Lay Lee Ong, who provided some of the history and closely examined both text and art to make sure the book would meet with Margret's exacting approval. And I, of course, am personally grateful that the great god of publishing took pity on me one fine October day and allowed me to rediscover one of the Reys' first books for children.

—*Anita Silvey*
Boston, Massachusetts